SPANISH IS THE LANGUAGE OF MY FAMILY

Michael Genhart

Illustrated by John Parra

NEAL PORTER BOOKS

HOLIDAY HOUSE / NEW YORK

Every year at my school there is a spelling bee in Spanish. I'm the first in my class to sign up because Spanish is the language of my family.

Es la lengua de mi familia.

DELETREO EN ESPAÑOL!

¡ k l m n ñ o (ó) p q r s t u (ú, ü) v w x y z

¡CONCURSO DE DELETREO
EN ESPAÑOL!

A B
C G
D
E
F

SPANISH SPELLING BEE
SIGN UP TODAY!

I already know how to spell many words.

Familia is family. F-a-m-i-l-i-a
Juntos is together. J-u-n-t-o-s
Corazón is heart. C-o-r-a-z-ó-n

C C C C C

I don't know how to spell some words yet.
My abuela helps me prepare.
Hay una lista de palabras.
We carefully review each word.

Hermoso is beautiful. H-e-r-m-o-s-o
Orgulloso is proud. O-r-g-u-l-l-o-s-o
Fuerte is strong. F-u-e-r-t-e

When she studies with me, my abuela shares stories
of when she was a little girl.
She tells me things were very different back then.
The rule at school was "English only."
Speaking Spanish was not allowed.
"Manolito, el español no estaba permitido," she explains.

It's hard to imagine not being allowed to speak Spanish.

Abuela tells me, "On the playground, we would sneak in Spanish."

"You did?" I ask.

"But we'd get in big trouble," Abuela continues. "If we ever got caught."

"¿Qué pasaba, Abu?"

"We were punished," she tells me. "And we were told that Spanish—and anyone who spoke it—was wrong, or worse."

"I was sent home for speaking Spanish to a classmate,"
Abuela remembers.
I feel so sad hearing this and her other stories.
"Your auntie, Tía Pancha, got spanked with a paddle for
every Spanish word she spoke.
And mi amiguita Kika had her mouth washed out
with soap for speaking Spanish."

Fea is ugly. F-e-a
Mala is bad. M-a-l-a
Sucia is dirty. S-u-c-i-a

Abuela and my family are not ugly, bad, or dirty.
¡Nuestra lengua no es mala!

I work even harder.
Practico y practico con mi abuela.
I must remember that some words
have special letters and accents.

Daño is harm. D-a-ñ-o
Por qué is why? P-o-r q-u-é
Bilingüe is bilingual. B-i-l-i-n-g-ü-e

I am climbing a high mountain.
I know I can reach the top,
just like I know I can win this spelling bee.
Tengo fuerza.

But studying all these words is hard.
Sometimes I get frustrated and tired.
Abuela makes me churros.
Mamá and Papá tell me jokes.

Delicioso is delicious. D-e-l-i-c-i-o-s-o
Risa is laughter. R-i-s-a
Apoyo is support. A-p-o-y-o

On the day of the contest,
my family gathers in the audience.
Their cheers give me confidence.
Me siento apoyado por ellos.
One by one, we are called up to spell.

My first word is poderoso.
I take a deep breath and begin.

P-o-d-e-r-o-s-o...powerful.
¡Abu es poderosísima!
I feel powerful, proud, and strong, just like Abu.

I spell more and more words correctly.
Then it's down to just two of us.

The word is vergüenza. V-e-r-g-ü-e-n-z-a

My schoolmate makes a spelling error.
I watch him walk slowly back to his chair.

Now it's my turn to spell the same word—shame.
I know about this from Abu.
Ay, ay, ay! I misspell it too!
We start again.

When my classmate spells the next word,
he leaves out a letter.
I can feel my heart beating faster.
I take another deep breath.
Whew! This time I get it right!

There's only one more word to go.
If I spell it right, I will win.
Respeto.
Como el respeto que tengo por Abu,
por mi familia,
y por mi lengua.

R-e-s-p-e-t-o

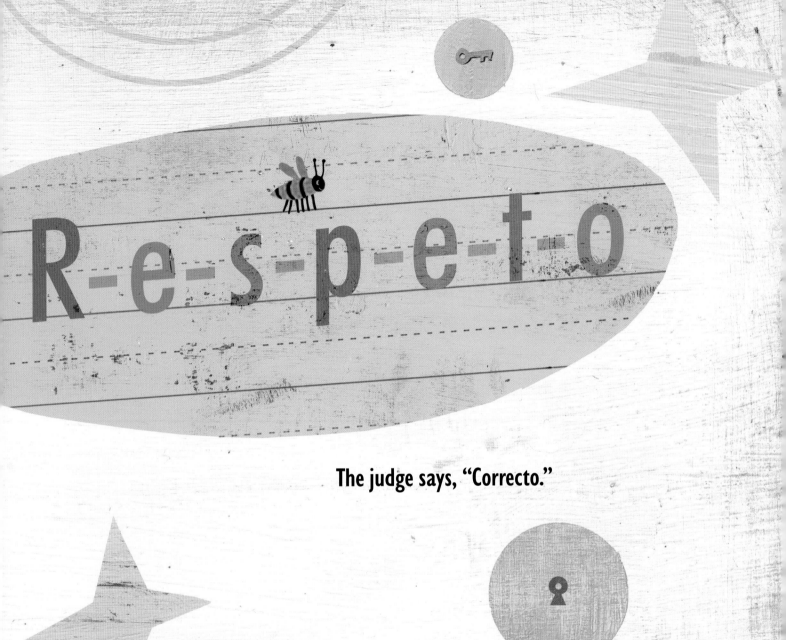

R-e-s-p-e-t-o

The judge says, "Correcto."

My family cheers!
My abuela is crying.
And at that moment, I know.
We both won today.

Abuela hugs me tight and says,
"¡Mi corazón! ¡Felicidades!"
"Te quiero mucho, Abu!" I say,
full of pride.

Triunfante is triumphant. T-r-i-u-n-f-a-n-t-e

Sanación is healing. S-a-n-a-c-i-ó-n

Amor is love. A-m-o-r

A NOTE FROM THE AUTHOR

A proud Mexican American family. My mother (older daughter), my aunt, and my grandparents. Southern California, 1943. (Personal collection)

When I was a child, my mother would tell me about not being able to speak her first language, Spanish, in public school in Southern California. She would tearfully point out how she and fellow students were humiliated and punished for speaking Spanish, although they naturally continued to use Spanish at home. However, as they grew up and had families of their own, my mother and many other parents of similar age did not speak Spanish with their children because they feared their children would suffer the same shaming. Consequently, in many families throughout the southwestern United States, there are generations of children and adults of Latin American heritage who do not speak Spanish. *Spanish Is the Language of My Family* is a story inspired by this period in U.S. history, particularly from the 1930s through the 1960s. I hope that through understanding this history, all children and adults of Latin American descent will feel pride in Spanish, the language of their families.

NATIONAL SPANISH SPELLING BEE

The first Concurso Nacional de Deletreo en Español, or National Spanish Spelling Bee, was held in Albuquerque, New Mexico, in 2011—with eleven contestants. Its founder and director, David Briseño, was inspired to start the Concurso Nacional by events from his parents' childhood. Like countless others, they were punished in school for speaking Spanish. They were belittled, spanked, or had their mouths washed out with soap if teachers caught them speaking their native language. As a result, Briseño did not grow up

speaking Spanish. His goal in founding the National Spanish Spelling Bee was to change the history of negative attitudes toward Spanish and to raise its status in the United States.

While New Mexico students have participated in state Spanish spelling bees since 1994, the National Spanish Spelling Bee is now over a decade old and has contestants representing fourteen states to date. Those who make it to the national level have first competed in state and regional contests. Students are given a "lista de palabras," a list of about 1,500 Spanish words to study and spell correctly, including any diacritical marks (e.g., tilde, diéresis, virgulilla). While many students are native Spanish speakers, native English speakers are increasingly drawn to this competition, reflecting the same interest in bilingual programs in schools across the country. And the Concurso Nacional itself is now held in different cities and states to reach larger audiences and gain more visibility.

PROHIBITING SPEAKING SPANISH IN PUBLIC SCHOOLS

The United States does not have an official language, even though English is the most commonly spoken one. Some people believe that speaking English is at the center of what it means to be an American. Underneath these beliefs are ideas that if someone moves here from another country, they should give up the customs and culture of the country they came from and learn English to be a "good American" or a "real" American citizen. Sadly, others believe there is no room for other cultures and languages (besides English) in this country.

Historically, Spanish—along with Native American languages—was spoken in the U.S. long before English. Just listen: Spanish words are everywhere in our everyday speech—calle (street), camino (road), mar (sea), plaza (plaza), and patio (patio). They are in the names of many U.S. cities and states, such as San Francisco, San Antonio, Los Angeles, El Paso,

Colorado, Nevada, and Florida. Today, people of Latin American heritage are the largest racial or minority group in the U.S., making Spanish the second most common language spoken at home by people five years and older.

Despite this ever-increasing presence of Latin American influence in U.S. culture, there has also been a long history of anti-Spanish and anti-Mexican feelings in this country. A key example of this was the "English only" laws and "no Spanish" rule that prevailed in southwestern American states (Arizona, California, Colorado, New Mexico, and Texas) for decades in the early to mid-twentieth century in accordance with state laws—with roots in the 1906 Naturalization Act, which required people applying to become U.S. citizens to be fluent in English, as well as laws circa 1918, which made English the language of instruction.

As noted earlier, during this time students who spoke Spanish in school were scolded, punished (including paying fines or serving detention), and humiliated. On occasion a "board of education" paddle was used to spank a child for every Spanish word that was spoken. Spanish was seen as a disability, not a strength. Denying Spanish in school made these kids feel like they were less than, and the impact of this shaming resulted in low self-esteem and self-worth, as well as a high dropout rate in schools. The accumulation of this emotional harm to multitudes of people of Latin American heritage is a kind of historical and generational trauma—one which will require time and effort to heal (including telling the story of what occurred).

This shameful period ended with the passage of Texas Senator Ralph Yarborough's Bilingual Education Act of 1968. In passing this law, which was later upheld by the Supreme Court in *Lau v. Nichols* (1974), federal support was granted to provide help for students with "limited English-speaking ability" by promoting their native languages and cultures while at the same time teaching them in English. It also meant that these minority students, who were underachieving in school because of "English only" laws, would finally be given a chance at an equal education. The Bilingual Education Act has been amended subsequently, including the No Child Left Behind Act (2001) and the Every Student Succeeds Act (2015), to reflect the changing needs of students and society.

Bilingual education in American public schools has, however, been controversial. Those who support bilingual education state that it opens opportunities to learn as well as boosts a student's self-esteem, while those against it suggest it contributes to a weaker education, gets in the way of learning English, or is anti-American. Politics, economics, and social climate all play a role in the back-and-forth battles to expand or diminish bilingual education programs in American public schools.

EL DÍA DE LOS NIÑOS / EL DÍA DE LOS LIBROS

While research continues regarding the strengths and weaknesses of bilingual education, public and school libraries across the U.S. have embraced literacy for children of all linguistic and cultural backgrounds in the springtime celebration known as El día de los niños/El día de los libros, or Día (Children's Day/Book Day). In 1997, author Pat Mora founded Día, which is celebrated on April 30 (the same as Children's Day in México) to link all children to books, languages, and cultures. Putting literacy at the center of this celebration, Mora and now the American Library Association's REFORMA (National Association to Promote Library and Information Services to Latinos and the Spanish Speaking) promote Día as the day to highlight the whole year's work—connecting children to "book joy," storytelling, writing their own books, and reading—honoring their home language as well as introducing them to the many languages they may not have heard before.

To my mamá, Rosita Teresa Castro Sánchez, who like many others endured this shaming. May this story offer healing and celebration. —M.G.

Dedicated to my aunt Irma —J.P.

SELECTED REFERENCES

Birdwell, Brian E., Andi McDaniel, Keenan Sloan, and Jennifer Smith. "When I Dream Dreams." Filmed 2001 at Trinity University. Video. https://archive.org/details/WhenIDreamDreams.

García, Ofelia, and Jo Anne Kleifgen. *Educating Emergent Bilinguals: Policies, Programs, and Practices for English Learners.* Teachers College Press, 2018.

Lozano, Rosina. *An American Language: The History of Spanish in the United States.* University of California Press, 2018.

Menchaca, Martha. *The Mexican Outsiders: A Community History of Marginalization and Discrimination in California.* University of Texas Press, 1995.

Tonatiuh, Duncan. *Separate Is Never Equal: Sylvia Mendez and Her Family's Fight for Desegregation.* Abrams Books for Young Readers, 2014.

Neal Porter Books

Text copyright © 2023 by Michael Genhart

Illustrations copyright © 2023 by John Parra

This book is being published simultaneously in Spanish as *El español es la lengua de mi familia.*

All Rights Reserved

HOLIDAY HOUSE is registered in the U.S. Patent and Trademark Office.

Printed and bound in March 2023 at RR Donnelley, Dongguan, China.

The artwork for this book was created using acrylic paint on illustration board and digital media.

Book design by Jennifer Browne

www.holidayhouse.com

First Edition

10 9 8 7 6 5 4 3 2 1

Library of Congress Cataloging-in-Publication Data

Names: Genhart, Michael, author. | Parra, John, illustrator.

Title: Spanish is the language of my family / by Michael Genhart ; illustrated by John Parra.

Description: First edition. | New York : Holiday House, [2023] | "A Neal Porter Book." | Includes bibliographical references and index. | Audience: Ages 4 to 8. | Audience: Grades K–1. | Includes some text in Spanish. | Summary: A young boy bonds with his beloved abuela over a love of Spanish.

Identifiers: LCCN 2022033724 | ISBN 9780823450046 (hardcover)

Subjects: CYAC: Spanish language—Fiction. | Grandmothers—Fiction. | Spelling bees—Fiction. | Hispanic Americans—Fiction. | LCGFT: Picture books.

Classification: LCC PZ7.1.G47 Sp 2023 | DDC [E]--dc23

LC record available at https://lccn.loc.gov/2022033724

ISBN: 978-0-8234-5004-6 (English hardcover)

ISBN: 978-0-8234-5446-4 (Spanish hardcover as *El español es la lengua de mi familia*)

THE SPANISH ALPHABET (el abecedario)*

Aa	Bb	Cc	Dd	Ee	Ff
a	be	ce	de	e	efe
Gg	**Hh**	**Ii**	**Jj**	**Kk**	**Ll**
ge	hache	i	jota	ka	ele
Mm	**Nn**	**Ññ**	**Oo**	**Pp**	**Qq**
eme	ene	eñe	o	pe	cu
Rr	**Ss**	**Tt**	**Uu**	**Vv**	**Ww**
ere	ese	te	u	ve	doble u
Xx	**Yy**	**Zz**			
equis	i griega	zeta			

*Sometimes letters combine in Spanish and produce unique pronunciations

such as two eles or "ll" (pronounced like "y" in English),

two eres or "rr" (pronounced with a trill or roll of the tongue), and "ch" (pronounced like "che").

Depending on the word, vowels (a,e,i,o,u) can have an accent mark (tilde).

With some words, a "u" will appear as "ü" (diéresis).